1

Magnificent Mabel
and the
Christmas Elf

At Christmas time I can't help being a sweety heart.

I am so kind and pleasant.

I love fairy lights.

I love doing carols by candlelight as long as people don't stare at me.

I especially love decorating the tree.

Every year Mum gets our box of decorations down from the

attic. That box is really dusty on the outside, but inside the Christmas decorations are shiny and new.

My favourite decoration is a naughty elf that is green and red. That naughty

elf lights up when you press a
button on its tummy.

Sometimes that naughty elf
winks at me when no one else is
looking.

Sometimes that naughty elf
speaks to me in a teeny-tiny
voice.

Whenever I press that
naughty elf's tummy I can't help
getting in the Christmas spirit.

My teacher Mr Messenger loves getting in the Christmas spirit too. He wears a red and white jumper with snowflakes on it and at Christmastime he isn't even strict.

Last Monday instead of teaching us maths and

reading, he let us make paper
chains all day long.

Mr Messenger says Class
One can't have too many paper
chains.

I think this is
quite a good
point of Mr
Messenger's,
but some

people in my class, e.g. Edward
Silitoe, don't like making paper
chains.

Last Monday Edward
Silitoe told Mr Messenger that
decorating Class One was not as
important as learning our times
tables.

Mr Messenger told Edward
Silitoe to get in the Christmas
spirit but Edward Silitoe did

not get in the Christmas spirit.
Edward Silitoe got on with his
maths.

I don't know why Edward
Silitoe finds it so tricky to get in
the Christmas spirit.

Getting in the
Christmas spirit

is EASY.

I looked at Edward Silitoe doing his maths and I smiled kindly.

"Edward Silitoe," I said. "Do you need help making paper chains?"

But Edward Silitoe said "No" in a grumpy voice and then Edward Silitoe scowled.

I did not scowl back.

I did not even poke Edward Silitoe a teeny bit hard in the tummy.

I cut out a snowflake for Edward Silitoe and I gave him a kind smile.

I was as good as gold.

This is what happens to me when I am in the Christmas spirit.

But this year on Christmas

Eve two things broke my Christmas spirit and those things were my sister Meg and the naughty Christmas elf.

I was in the kitchen, making snowflakes.

I had to use old newspaper for my snowflakes instead of fresh paper because SOME people in my family are mad about recycling.

But I did not mind.

I thought, at Christmas it is good to care about our planet.

I felt SO happy.

Even when Dad accidentally

pushed past me and knocked my snowflakes on the floor, I did not get cross with him.

I smiled politely and said, "Please may you be careful of my snowflakes if that is OK with you."

When Dad laughed and said, "What's got into Mabel?" I did not get cross. I stayed calm in a crisis.

"Dad," I said. "I am in the Christmas spirit. That is my point."

At that moment Meg came skipping into the kitchen. She was carrying a heavy bag.

Meg put that heavy bag down on the table.

I looked carefully at that bag of Meg's.

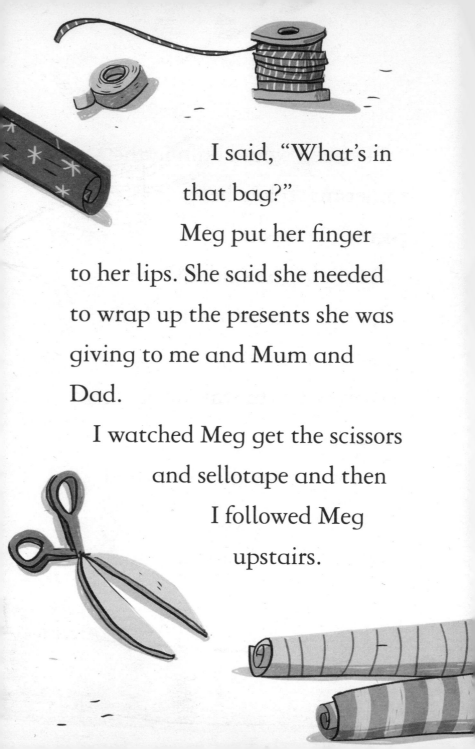

I said, "What's in
that bag?"

Meg put her finger
to her lips. She said she needed
to wrap up the presents she was
giving to me and Mum and
Dad.

I watched Meg get the scissors
and sellotape and then
I followed Meg
upstairs.

But Meg would
not let me follow her
into her bedroom.

"Mabel," she said, all
chirpety. "You're not allowed
to see what I am giving you.
You will have to wait until
tomorrow."

So I went downstairs to find
Mum.

I told Mum that it was time

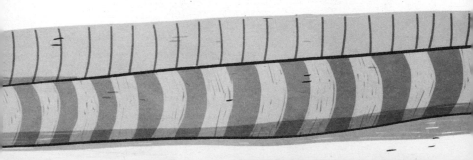

for me to wrap up MY presents.

'Where are they anyway?" I
said.

Mum sighed and looked at me
for a long time.

"Mabel," she said. "I took you
Christmas shopping with Meg
last week but you didn't want
to spend your pocket money on
presents. You spent it on that
toy stethoscope for

yourself instead."

Mum gave me her firm look. "Remember?" she said.

I gave Mum a firm look back.

I thought, somebody should remind that mother of mine that when it comes to shopping

I am not very sensible.

I thought, I don't even LIKE that stethoscope.

At that moment Meg came downstairs and put her presents under the tree.

There was one for Mum, one for Dad and one for me.

"I can't wait until tomorrow," said Meg.

I thought, it is all right for

some.

I thought, that sister of mine is so boasty.

That night we left mince pies and beer out for Father Christmas and we also left some chocolate biscuits because not everyone likes mince pies.

After that, Dad read us some Christmas stories and we all went to bed.

Except I did not go to sleep because it was Christmas the next day and I did not have any presents to give to anyone.

That's when I had a good idea.

I remembered about my family being keen on recycling.

I thought, what if I recycle my old stuff and give it to them?

I hopped out of bed and I

started to find old things to give away as presents.

I thought about giving Meg my doll called Annabel but then I remembered that Annabel might miss me too much so I put Annabel back in my bed and found Polly instead. Polly has a bald patch in the middle of her hair and a twisty leg. I thought, Meg will LOVE Polly.

I found a book of word searches for Dad and it looked practically new because I never do word searches if I can help it. I found an old bracelet that

is a bit too pink for me and I
thought, that is perfect for Mum
because she loves jewellery and
also she doesn't mind pink.

I laid all three presents on my

bed.

I could not wait to put them under the tree.

I felt so kind and generous.

I waited until everybody was definitely asleep and then I

waited a bit longer because even though I know Father Christmas is a kind and pleasant man, I did not fancy bumping into him in the middle of the night.

A long time later, when my lighting-up clock said it was midnight, I crept downstairs and tiptoed across the hall into the sitting room.

The tree was all twinkly.

Straightaway I could tell
that Father Christmas had been
because he had eaten the mince
pie AND the chocolate biscuits
and there were HUNDREDS of
presents under the tree.

I thought, I'm not going to
touch them.

I thought, I am

SUCH a good girl.

I placed my presents for Meg, Mum and Dad carefully under the tree and I started tiptoeing out of the room.

But when I looked back at the presents mine looked all wrong because they were not wrapped up.

I thought, someone should be helping me wrap those presents.

At that moment I spotted the naughty elf on the branch of the tree.

That naughty elf winked at me.

Then that naughty elf jumped down from its branch.

I did not say one word.

I was SHOCKED.

That naughty elf spoke to me in his teeny-tiny voice. He told me to BORROW a little bit of

paper from each present so I would have something to wrap MY presents in.

That elf told me to get a move on.

One thing I did not know
about elves is that they are
VERY BOSSY.

I could not help doing what
that elf said.

I tried tearing off a teeny bit
of paper from one of the presents
but the problem was, the paper
kept ripping.

I kept accidentally opening
whole entire presents. I tried not

to look at them because that is called cheating but it was hard not to notice because some of them were AMAZING.

But then I got a bit worried.

I thought, this is not right.

I told that elf to stop misbehaving and then I told him to get back to his branch.

I said if he did not do what I said, I would write a letter

to Father Christmas (I do not
normally like to tell tales
but this was an emergency
situation).

Then when the naughty elf
ignored me I shouted at him

REALLY, REALLY loudly.

That's when I heard footsteps coming down the stairs.

That's also when the naughty elf leapt back on to his branch.

Meg raced into the sitting room, all worried.

"Mabel!" she said, staring at the terrible mess. "What have you done?"

I looked at Meg firmly.

"Meg," I said. "If you think this is MY mess you are wrong. This is not my mess. This is not even my fault. That naughty Christmas elf made me open all the presents and he would not listen to me."

Then I had to stop speaking because my voice went all squeaky and my lip went a bit wobbly too.

I said, "That is the whole truth."

I said, "I don't know what to do."

Meg made a frowny face.

"Don't worry, Mabel," she said. "Come and help me wrap everything back up again."

I looked up at Meg to check she was not cross because when someone is cross I do not actually feel like helping them.

But Meg was too busy finding the sellotape to be cross so I said, "OK" and then I helped Meg wrap the presents back up. I could not quite remember which present went with which wrapping but Meg

said it didn't matter.

I even managed to use bits of leftover wrapping paper to wrap up the presents I was giving to Meg, Mum and Dad.

When everything was wrapped again, I gave that naughty elf a firm look. Then me and Meg held hands and tiptoed upstairs. Meg asked if I wanted to sleep with her in

her bed and I said yes because
I could tell that Meg was quite
lonely.

The next morning it was

Christmas Day.

Me and Meg raced downstairs. We had pancakes in our pyjamas and then we sat around the tree to open our presents.

I kept glaring at that elf but he pretended that nothing had happened.

I thought, that elf has got away with it.

I thought, that elf is SO

lucky.

I got LOADS of good presents, e.g. lighting-up trainers and a pottery set, but my best present was from Meg and it was a magic wand.

I thought, that sister of mine is QUITE KIND.

Then I remembered about MY presents.

I gave Mum the bracelet and

I gave Dad the word search book but I did not give Meg her present.

I stomped upstairs instead.

In my bedroom I spotted Annabel. She looked VERY precious.

I thought, Meg would probably prefer Annabel to Polly because Meg is quite greedy.

I thought, why do I have to

have such a greedy sister?

I wrapped Annabel up in Polly's old paper and I stomped back downstairs and gave her to Meg.

Meg went all

gaspy. She said "Thank you!"
with sparkling eyes. She gave
me a hug.

But I did not hug Meg back.

I glared at that naughty
Christmas elf.

I said, "This is all your fault" in a teeny-weeny voice that no one else could hear. I said, "You are SO naughty."

2

Magnificent Mabel
and the
Interesting Day
at School

The problem with school is that it is always the sameish.

This is because my teacher Mr Messenger is not keen on change. Like, for instance, when I brought all my teddies into school FOR A CHANGE Mr Messenger said teddies don't belong in Class One.

He said the teddies had to stay in the lost-property cupboard for the whole day.

The lost-property cupboard in our classroom is dark and cobwebby.

The lost-property cupboard is not a suitable place for my teddies.

But when I tried to explain this to Mr Messenger he said,

"That's enough, Mabel."

When Mr Messenger says, "That's enough, Mabel" he is not even joking.

These days it is not worth bringing teddies into school so I have to think of other things that will make school feel less sameish and more interesting.

Last week I thought it would make A NICE CHANGE if I

became a Spanish girl called
Maria Dolores for the day.

Maria Dolores doesn't
actually understand English.
When she came to school, Maria
Dolores couldn't understand Mr
Messenger when he asked her to
do her handwriting. She couldn't
understand one word of maths.
Maria Dolores was mostly keen
on waving her flamenco fan with

a red lace
fringe that
was made of silk
and came from
Barcelona in
Spain.

But Mr Messenger did not
admire Maria Dolores or her
flamenco fan.

Mr Messenger said that if
Maria Dolores didn't put her

flamenco fan away and switch
back to being Mabel Chase
AT ONCE then Maria Dolores
would have to go and sit outside
the headteacher's office.

Sitting outside the
headteacher's office makes your
tummy feel sick.

Sitting outside the
headteacher's office is worse
than eating chicken casserole for

supper.

That is why I had to stop being Maria Dolores and turn back into me, Mabel Chase.

That is why school is nearly

always the sameish.

But today I got all excited because something different happened.

At register Mr Messenger told us that a new boy called Jordi Bhogal was joining our class.

Mr Messenger said we must all be very kind and welcoming to Jordi Bhogal.

This made me all jumpy and

happy because being kind and welcoming is something I can do off by heart.

I thought, I will be Jordi

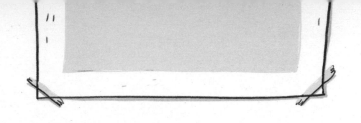

Bhogal's new friend.

I thought, I hope Mr
Messenger puts Jordi Bhogal
next to me.

But Mr Messenger put Jordi
Bhogal next to Harry Cox.

This is the whole tragedy of
my life.

I told Mr Messenger that
Harry Cox is not a kind and
welcoming boy. I said I was

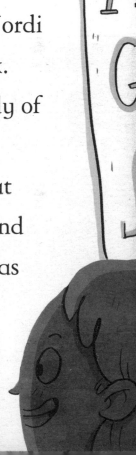

worried that Jordi Bhogal would be shy and frightened with a boy like Harry Cox. I explained that Jordi Bhogal would probably prefer to sit with me, Mabel Chase, because I know exactly how to be kind and welcoming.

But Mr Messenger did not hear one word. He opened a book and started to read us a story. I am now wondering if

maybe Mr Messenger is a teeny
bit deaf.

At break time Harry Cox took
Jordi Bhogal outside to play
football.

One thing I am not keen on is
football.

Playing football is not a kind
and welcoming thing to do.

I could tell that Jordi Bhogal
was putting on a brave face.

Putting on a brave face is
what you do when you don't
want anyone to know you are
shy and scared.

I could tell that Jordi Bhogal
needed rescuing so I put on my
kind and welcoming smile and
I marched over to that football

goal.

I told Jordi Bhogal all about my secret gold mine in the muddy patch at the back of the playground.

I told him that I could show him where to find the best bits of gold.

I said that we would definitely become millionaires and get in the newspaper.

I smiled in a kind and welcoming way the whole time I was speaking to Jordi Bhogal.

But Jordi Bhogal did not notice my kind and welcoming smile.

He was not interested in my gold mine.

He didn't care about being a millionaire.

Jordi Bhogal said, "I'm

playing football" and kicked the ball to Harry Cox.

I thought, I'll have to think of something REALLY exciting if I am going to get Jordi Bhogal away from Harry Cox.

I thought, living creatures are exciting.

I thought, I wonder if Jordi Bhogal likes ants.

I spent AGES searching for

rare and tiny ants in the spikey
grass next to my gold mine. I
put the ants in my pencil case
to keep them safe and I went to
find Jordi Bhogal.

Jordi Bhogal was playing
"it" with lots of other children.
Everyone was shouting.

I thought, all that noisy shouting must be scary for a new boy like Jordi Bhogal on his first day.

I thought, I'll just go and cheer him up.

I walked up to Jordi Bhogal and I said, "Do you want to see my ant zoo?" and I opened my pencil case.

Jordi Bhogal laughed and

made a face.

He said, "Gross." He said,
"Ants bite." Then he ran away.

This was actually quite rude
of Jordi Bhogal but I didn't get
cross and stampy because
I knew that Jordi
Bhogal was probably
nervous
and

shy and when people are nervous and shy they can be rude without meaning to be.

Like last year, when I was nervous and shy about being a bridesmaid at a smart wedding, the pageboy told me I looked like a pink marshmallow and I slightly stamped on his foot even though I didn't mean to.

I went away to think of

something that would stop Jordi
Bhogal being nervous and shy.

That's when I thought of a
circus.

I am mad about circuses.
When I grow up I would like to
be in one. I will juggle fire and,
also, I will be a tightrope walker.

Circuses are my best thing.

I thought, Jordi Bhogal may
not be keen on gold mines

or living
creatures but
I bet he likes
tightrope walking.
I thought, everybody likes
tightrope walking.
I thought, tightrope walking

will definitely stop Jordi Bhogal feeling nervous and shy. Also, tightrope walking will get Jordi Bhogal away from Harry Cox.

At lunchtime I headed straight for the metal fence next to the climbing frame because the top rail is EXACTLY like a tightrope. I climbed on top of that fence and then I stood up. It was a bit slippery and wobbly

but that was not a problem for
me because slippery and wobbly
is normal for a tightrope.

I set off down that tightrope.

I called out to Jordi Bhogal.

I said, "Tightrope walking is
SO fun."

I said, "I'm practising my circus skills."

I said, "Do you want to have a go?"

I gave Jordi Bhogal an especially kind and welcoming

smile.

Then I fell off and landed on my arm.

"OW!" I shouted, in a really loud voice because my arm hurt a lot.

I thought, now my tightrope career is over and it's all Jordi Bhogal's fault.

I thought, this is what comes from being kind and welcoming.

I sent Harry Cox to fetch Mrs Woodlea.

Mrs Woodlea is sometimes the school nurse and sometimes she helps out in Class One and sometimes she teaches PE.

Mrs Woodlea took me into my classroom and looked at my arm. She told me it was bruised.

She said the bruising was quite bad.

This made me feel quite cross and sometimes when I get cross I get tears in my eyes.

I glared at Mrs Woodlea and said, "This has not been a good

day."

I thought, poor me.

"What else has gone wrong today, Mabel?" asked Mrs Woodlea, and because Mrs Woodlea asked in a kind voice instead of being all nosy,

I told her about Harry Cox whisking the new boy Jordi Bhogal away from me in front of my eyes. I explained that instead of being a fun and interesting day it was now just another sameish day like all the others, except now I had a badly bruised arm as well.

"I only like school when interesting things happen to

me," I said grumpily.

Then I stopped talking to
Mrs Woodlea and got a slightly
wobbly lip.

Mrs Woodlea gave me a nice
smile and looked closely at my
arm.

She said, "You know, Mabel,
the bruising on your arm is
extremely interesting."

I looked at Mrs Woodlea out

of the corner of my eye to check
she wasn't being nice on purpose.
Because when grown-ups are
nice on purpose it doesn't count.

"Is it?" I asked in a small
voice.

"Hmmmm," said Mrs
Woodlea. "I've never seen
bruising quite like it." Then she
looked at my arm even more
closely and said, "I think you

might need a sling."

At that moment I made a big gasp and my lip stopped wobbling because one thing I have always wanted is a sling on my arm.

Mrs Woodlea said, "If you have a sling, everybody will know your arm is badly bruised and they will be careful not to bump into you."

I thought, I'm so glad Mrs Woodlea is our school nurse.

I thought, I've waited my whole life for this moment.

Mrs Woodlea pulled a white sling out of the first-aid box and put it carefully over my head. Then she laid my badly bruised arm gently in the white sling.

She said, "There you go, Mabel."

She said, "That should do the trick."

When I walked back out into the playground, everybody

turned and looked at my white sling.

Even Harry Cox and Jordi Bhogal stopped playing football and came over to have a closer look.

EVERYBODY asked what had happened to my arm.

And when I told them about my tightrope accident, EVERYBODY listened.

After lunch break we went
back to our classroom and I
told Mr Messenger all about my
badly bruised arm.

Mr Messenger agreed that

the bruising was extremely
interesting. Mr Messenger
said he thought I was VERY
brave. Mr Messenger asked me
if I could write with my badly
bruised arm.

I had a good think about this.

I tried to pick up a pencil but
the problem was I couldn't even
lift it. I shook my head. "Sorry,
Mr Messenger," I said. "My arm

is a bit too badly bruised to do writing."

Mr Messenger made his eyes all twinkly.

"Is that right?" said Mr Messenger. "Well then, you won't be able to do this afternoon's spelling test.

You'll have to go and sit in the reading corner instead."

The reading corner in Class One has cushions and beanbags.

The reading corner is the nicest place in school.

I tried not to smile but this was quite hard because I felt so happy about missing the spelling test. I sucked in my cheeks and nodded politely at

Mr Messenger and I held my
badly bruised arm very carefully
as I went over to the reading
corner.

I stroked my white sling and
I watched Harry Cox and Jordi
Bhogal and everybody

else in Class One do the boring spelling test.

I thought, school isn't always the sameish.

School is sometimes REALLY interesting.

3

Magnificent Mabel
and the
Toddler Cousin

I don't know why everyone
thinks looking after a baby is
hard work.

Looking after a baby is EASY.
Looking after a baby is FUN.
That's why I was so happy
last Saturday when
Mum told me
and my sister
Meg that
our cousin

William was coming to visit.

"That's fine by me," I said. "Because William is a baby and I am brilliant with babies."

Mum said that William isn't a baby any more, he is a toddler.

"Toddlers are fine by me too," I said. "I am not even fussy. Looking after toddlers is easy and fun."

"Mabel," said my sister Meg.

"Toddlers are really HARD WORK and exhausting."

I told Meg that she had got her facts wrong and waited for Mum to agree with me but Mum did not agree with me.

Mum agreed with Meg.

"Meg's right," said Mum. "Toddlers are REALLY HARD WORK. That's why Auntie Carrie and Uncle Lawrence are always EXHAUSTED."

I thought, that's strange.

When I look after toddlers I don't feel tired.

I can look after toddlers

without thinking.

Then Mum told us that Auntie Carrie and Uncle Lawrence needed a rest from running around after William all the time so they were leaving him with us to look after for a whole night.

Mum said me and Meg had to be REALLY good and helpful.

I was just thinking that

being good and helpful is not a problem for me when Meg ruined everything.

She went all flibberty and said, "Ooh, Mum. Can I play with William and feed him snacks and can I read him a bedtime story too?"

This made me want to poke Meg a teeny bit hard in the tummy because I am the one

who is brilliant with babies in
this house.

I don't even find toddlers
exhausting.

I find toddlers easy and fun.

Also, I was planning to read
William a bedtime story.

I thought, why is my sister
SUCH a copycat?

But I couldn't poke Meg a
teeny bit hard in the tummy

because Mum was watching me.

So I kicked Meg slightly gently on the foot instead. Then I stomped off to my room before I had to say sorry.

In my room I had the good idea of making a long list of all the things I could do when William arrived.

It took me nearly the whole day.

I thought, I don't know
what Auntie Carrie and Uncle
Lawrence would do without me.
I thought, where are they

anyway?

But then the doorbell rang and it was Auntie Carrie and Uncle Lawrence and they were carrying our cousin William and they were also carrying a lot of bags.

Luckily William didn't have a snotty nose and porridge round his mouth like some toddlers do.

William had pink cheeks and

 fluffy hair and
bright brown eyes.
William was
just my kind of
toddler.

I was just about to say hello
when Meg rushed up and
said, "Hello, William. Hello,
William" over and over again in
a silly voice.

William did not say hello

back.

William bashed Meg on the
nose.

I thought, that's what
happens when you speak in a
silly voice.

But Auntie Carrie and Uncle
Lawrence did not notice that
William was not keen on Meg.

They were too busy giving
Mum and Dad a long list of

instructions about how to look after William.

I tried telling everybody that we didn't need a long list of instructions because I am brilliant with toddlers but none of those grown-ups let me get a word in edgeways, not even when I kept interrupting and talking in a really loud voice.

They just said, "Shhhh" and,

"In a minute, Mabel", and Mum
gave me another of her looks.

Then Auntie Carrie and Uncle
Lawrence kissed William and
said goodbye.

They had only been gone for one tiny millisecond when Meg said, "Can I play with William now?" and Mum said yes.

Sometimes life isn't even fair.

Meg took William into the living room and sat down on the sofa.

She started to play the horsey game with him.

She would not wipe that smile

off her face.

Except William was NOT SMILING.

William was wriggling and trying to get away.

William was going purple in the face.

William was PRACTICALLY CRYING.

Anyone could see that William needed rescuing

STRAIGHTAWAY.

I dashed upstairs to change
into my superhero costume
because my superhero costume is
suitable for most rescue missions,
even ones involving toddlers.

I flew down the stairs and I
swooshed into the living room
faster than a rocket.

I smashed into everything
on my way (because

smashing into things is what
superheroes do on a daily basis).

I dived towards Meg and I
bashed into her.

I had to bash quite hard

because when you're a superhero you don't know your own strength.

Meg said, "Ouch!" and let go of William in a jiffy.

William was so happy to be free. He stopped crying and swooshed after me at toppity speed.

I thought, William is a superhero like me.

I thought, that's a
nice surprise.

Me and William
went on a mission
together.

We rescued a real-
live ladybird.

We saved a miniature
puppy. We leapt

off tall buildings. Then Mum raced in from the kitchen. "Mabel!" she said. "STOP CHARGING AROUND!" This made me quite cross.

"I am not charging," I said.
"Superheroes don't charge. I was
saving lives."

Mum put her hands on her
hips.

When Mum puts her hands on
her hips, she means business.

"Mabel," she said. "Go and
be a superhero in the garden
instead."

"No thank you very much, madam," I said, because that is called being polite and being polite sometimes works.

But it didn't work because Mum said "Mabel" in a MUCH CROSSER voice and held open the back door.

So I stomped outside.

It was cold in the garden and I did not have a coat.

I thought, I'm going to catch hypothermia if that family of mine is not careful.

I thought, I'll just sneak back in.

But when I sneaked back in I could not believe what I was seeing.

Meg was back on the sofa with William and she was feeding him a biscuit.

I was so shocked.

"You can't give biscuits to babies," I said. "Biscuits are not suitable for babies. Babies should only eat HEALTHY food."

But nobody listened to me.

I thought, I'm going to make something healthy for that cousin of mine.

I went into the kitchen and put on my apron.

I found carrots and broccoli and an old parsnip in the fridge and I popped them into the food blender.

I thought, it's a good job
someone in this family knows
what toddlers should eat.

I thought, I'll whizz these up
in a jiffy.

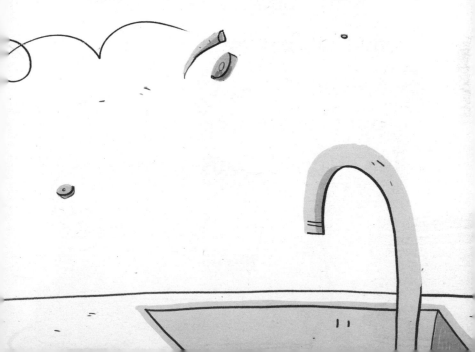

Except it wasn't my fault that no one was around to remind me to put the lid on the blender.

William's healthy snacks flew around the kitchen at a million miles an hour.

Dad raced into the kitchen and shouted, "Mabel" in a really loud voice.

When Dad shouts it gives me a headache.

That's why I had to race up to my room and slam the door tight shut and put my head under my duvet.

But then I heard something that made my heart go all

sinky.

It was not Dad shouting. It
was the sound of crying and
it was coming from the spare
room.

I thought, what now?

I marched down the landing
and I burst into the spare room.

William was in his travel
cot and Mum and Meg were
standing over him.

Mum put her fingers up to her lips. She said, "Shhhh." She said, "We're trying to get William to go down for a nap. Meg is reading him a bedtime story."

I could tell in less than a millisecond that William did NOT like Meg's type of reading.

When my sister reads she doesn't do voices or actions. She doesn't even add her own made-up words. She just says what is on the page.

Meg's type of reading is very slow and careful.

William snatched that book

out of Meg's hand and threw it at her.

The book hit Meg on the forehead.

"Ow!" said Meg, and her face went pink.

Then something quite bad happened. Meg's face went pinker

than ever and she started to cry.

When Meg cries it makes
me want to cry too. Big sisters
should not cry.

I thought, that baby is a
menace.

I thought, that sister of mine
needs my help.

I went over to our baby cousin
and leaned over the travel cot.

I put on my strictest voice and

said, "Stop throwing books or you'll wake up the lion."

Then I roared very, very loudly, just like a real lion, to show William that I meant business.

William stopped crying. He
looked at me for a long time
and then. . .

. . . he laughed.

I did not laugh back.

I picked up Meg's book and I

started to read a bedtime story.

I was not slow and careful. I did all the voices and actions.

I left out all the boring bits and added lots of my own story too.

I read that whole book in less than two minutes and I didn't even look at the words.

It was SO easy.

William did not try to grab

the book out of my hands and throw it. He didn't shout or scream and he didn't bash me on the nose either.

He listened.

Then when I finished, he said, "MO!"

So I had to keep telling that story over and over again until eventually William rubbed his eyes and fell asleep.

Everyone was SO pleased with me.

Meg stopped crying and gave me a hug.

Mum said I was brilliant with babies.

Dad said, "Thank goodness for Mabel."

We all crept out of the spare room and went downstairs for a biscuit.

"See," I said munching away. "Looking after babies is easy."

Mum, Dad and Meg winked at each other.

One thing I'm not keen on is people winking at each other.

Winking is RUDE.

"Oh good," said Dad, smiling at me. "Then you'll still have plenty of energy to help us tidy up all this mess."

I stopped munching my biscuit and I stopped feeling chirpy too.

I thought, how rude.

I glared at Dad and I glared at Mum and I slightly elbowed Meg in the tummy.

Tidying is not easy or fun.

When it comes to tidying I am not full of beans.

I did a bit of a yawn.

"Actually," I said, "William is not as easy as babies are because William is a toddler."

I said, "Toddlers are really hard work and I am exhausted." I said, "I'll just have a little lie down."